Abuela

by *Arthur Dorros*

illustrated by *Elisa Kleven*

PUFFIN BOOKS

PUFFIN BOOKS
Published by the Penguin Group
Penguin Books USA Inc., 375 Hudson Street, New York, New York 10014, U.S.A.
Penguin Books Ltd, 27 Wrights Lane, London W8 5TZ, England
Penguin Books Australia Ltd, Ringwood, Victoria, Australia
Penguin Books Canada Ltd, 10 Alcorn Avenue, Toronto, Ontario, Canada M4V 3B2
Penguin Books (N.Z.) Ltd, 182-190 Wairau Road, Auckland 10, New Zealand

Penguin Books Ltd, Registered Offices: Harmondsworth, Middlesex, England

First published in the United States of America by Dutton Children's Books,
a division of Penguin Books USA Inc., 1991
Published in Puffin Books, 1997

1 3 5 7 9 10 8 6 4 2

THE LIBRARY OF CONGRESS HAS CATALOGED THE DUTTON EDITION AS FOLLOWS:
Dorros, Arthur.
Abuela / by Arthur Dorros; illustrated by Elisa Kleven.
p.   cm.
Summary: While riding on a bus with her grandmother,
a little girl imagines that they are carried up into the sky
and fly over the sights of New York City.
ISBN 0-525-44750-4
[1. Imagination—Fiction. 2. Flight—Fiction. 3. Hispanic Americans—Fiction.
4. Grandmothers—Fiction. 5. New York (N.Y.)—Fiction.] I. Kleven, Elisa, ill.
II. Title. PZ7.D7294Ab 1991
[E]—dc20   90-21459 CIP AC

Puffin Books ISBN 0-14-056225-7

Printed in the U.S.A.

To my grandmothers, *a mis abuelas*, and Alex

—A.D.

For my nephews, Sam, Joey, Jacob, Andrew,
Sean, Todd, Harry, and Scott

—E.K.

Abuela takes me on the bus.
We go all around the city.

Abuela is my grandma.
She is my mother's mother.
Abuela means "grandma" in Spanish.
Abuela speaks mostly Spanish because
that's what people spoke where she grew up,
before she came to this country.
Abuela and I are always going places.

Today we're going to the park.
"*El parque es lindo,*" says Abuela.
I know what she means.
I think the park is beautiful too.

"*Tantos pájaros*," Abuela says
as a flock of birds surrounds us.
So many birds.
They're picking up the bread we brought.

What if they picked me up
and carried me
high above the park?
What if I could fly?
Abuela would wonder where I was.
Swooping like a bird, I'd call to her.

Then she'd see me flying.
Rosalba the bird.
"*Rosalba el pájaro*," she'd say.
"*Ven, Abuela*. Come, Abuela," I'd say.
"*Sí, quiero volar*," Abuela would reply
as she leaped into the sky
with her skirt flapping in the wind.

We would fly all over the city.
"*Mira*," Abuela would say, pointing.

And I'd look, as we soared
over parks and streets, dogs and people.

We'd wave to the people waiting for the bus.
"*Buenos días*," we'd say.
"*Buenos días*. Good morning," they'd call
up to us.
We'd fly over factories and trains...

and glide close to the sea.
"Cerca del mar," we'd say.
We'd almost touch the tops of waves.

Abuela's skirt would be a sail.
She could race with the sailboats.
I'll bet she'd win.

We'd fly to where the ships are docked,
and watch people unload fruits
from the land where Abuela grew up.
Mangos, bananas, papayas—
those are all Spanish words.
So are rodeo, patio, and burro.
Maybe we'd see a cousin of Abuela's
hooking boxes of fruit to a crane.
We saw her cousin Daniel once,
unloading and loading the ships.

Out past the boats in the harbor
we'd see the Statue of Liberty.
"Me gusta," Abuela would say.
Abuela really likes her.
I do too.
We would circle around Liberty's head
and wave to the people visiting her.
That would remind Abuela of when
she first came to this country.

"*Vamos al aeropuerto*," she'd say.
She'd take me to the airport where
the plane that first brought her landed.
"*Cuidado*," Abuela would tell me.
We'd have to be careful
as we went for a short ride.

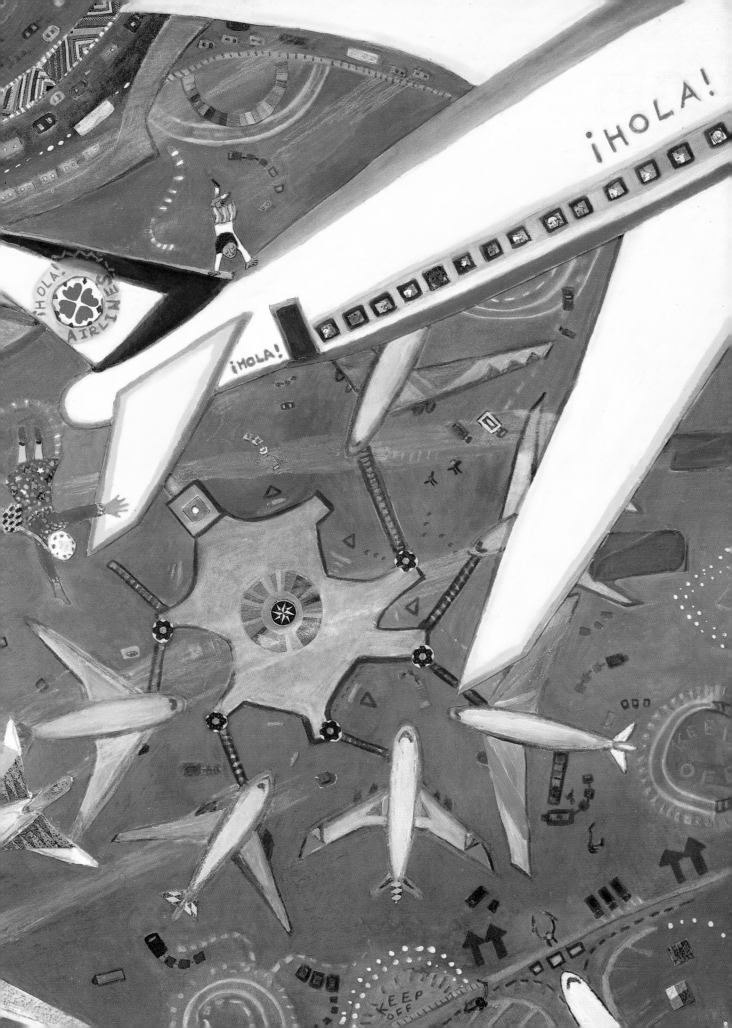

Then we could fly to *tío* Pablo's
and *tía* Elisa's store.
Pablo is my uncle, my *tío*,
and Elisa is my aunt, my *tía*.
They'd be surprised when we flew in,
but they'd offer us a cool *limonada*.
Flying is hot work.
"*Pero quiero volar más*,"
Abuela would say.
She wants to fly more.
I want to fly more too.

We could fly to *las nubes*, the clouds.
One looks like a cat, *un gato*.
One looks like a bear, *un oso*.
One looks like a chair, *una silla*.
"Descansemos un momento,"
Abuela would say.
She wants to rest a moment.
We would rest in our chair,
and Abuela would hold me in her arms,
with the whole sky
our house, *nuestra casa*.

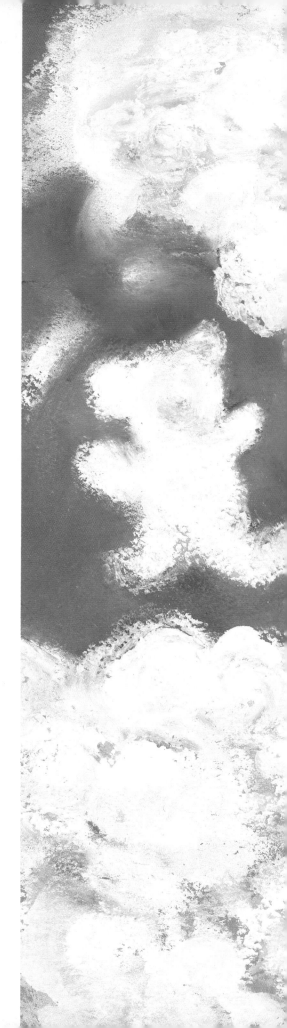

We'd be as high as airplanes,
balloons, and birds,
and higher than the tall buildings downtown.
But we'd fly there too
to look around.

We could find the building
where my father works.

"*Hola, papá,*" I'd say as I waved.
And Abuela would do a flip for fun
as we passed by the windows.

"*Mira,*" I hear Abuela say.
"Look," she's telling me.

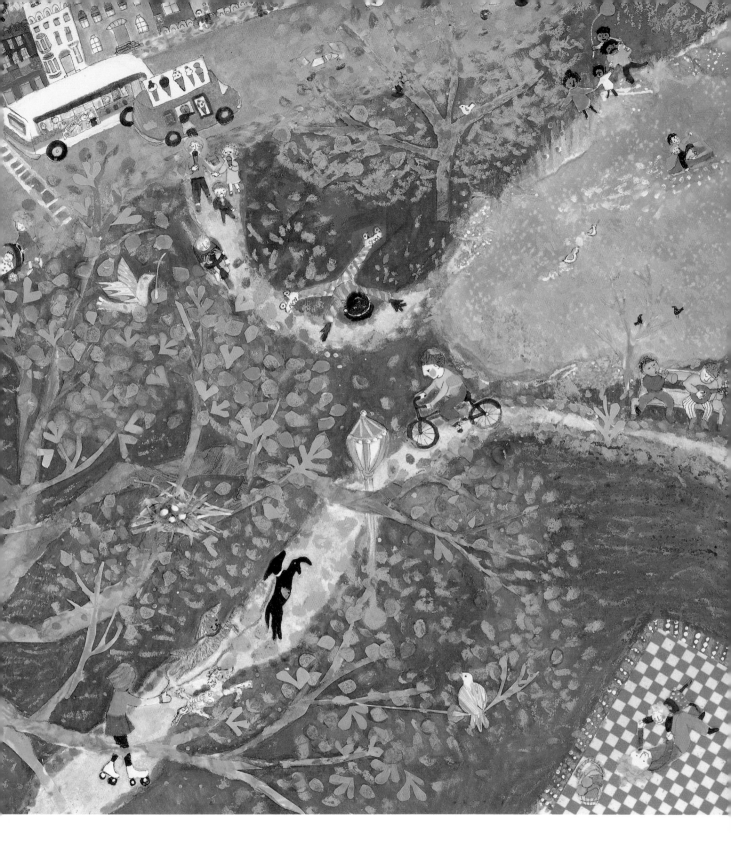

I do look,
and we are back in the park.

We are walking by the lake.
Abuela probably wants to go for a boat ride.
"*Vamos a otra aventura,*" she says.
She wants us to go for another adventure.
That's just one of the things I love
about Abuela.
She likes adventures.

Abuela takes my hand.
"*Vamos*," she says.
"Let's go."

Glossary

Abuela (ah-BWEH-lah)   Grandmother

Buenos días (BWEH-nohs DEE-ahs)   Good day

Cerca del mar (SEHR-kah dehl mahr)   Close to the sea

Cuidado (kwee-DAH-doh)   Be careful

Descansemos un momento (dehs-kahn-SEH-mohs oon moh-MEHN-toh)
    Let's rest a moment

El parque es lindo (ehl PAHR-kay ehs LEEN-doh)
    The park is beautiful

Hola, papá (OH-lah, pah-PAH)   Hello, papa

Las nubes (lahs NOO-behs)   The clouds

Limonada (lee-moh-NAH-dah)   Lemonade

Me gusta (meh GOO-stah)   I like

Mira (MEE-rah)   Look

Nuestra casa (NWEH-strah CAH-sah)   Our house

Pero quiero volar más (PEH-roh key-EH-roh boh-LAR mahs)
    But I would like to fly more

Rosalba el pájaro (roh-SAHL-bah ehl PAH-hah-roh)
    Rosalba the bird

Sí, quiero volar (see, key-EH-roh boh-LAR)
    Yes, I want to fly

Tantos pájaros (TAHN-tohs PAH-hah-rohs)   So many birds

Tía (TEE-ah)   Aunt

Tío (TEE-oh)   Uncle

Un gato (oon GAH-toh)   A cat

Un oso (oon OH-soh)   A bear

Una silla (OON-ah SEE-yah)   A chair

Vamos (BAH-mohs)   Let's go

Vamos al aeropuerto (BAH-mohs ahl ah-ehr-oh-PWEHR-toh)
    Let's go to the airport

Vamos a otra aventura (BAH-mohs ah OH-trah ah-behn-TOO-rah)
    Let's go on another adventure

Ven (behn)   Come

The capitalized syllable is stressed in pronunciation.